Wooing the Dragon

A Play by
Matthew Johnson

Wooing The Dragon

Published by Untold Stories

Riverside, California

This is a work of fiction. Names, characters, businesses, places, events, and incidents are either the products of the author's imagination or used in a fictitious manner. Any resemblance to actual persons, living or dead, or actual events is purely coincidental.

For rights to perform the play, contact the author at writerman84@gmail.com.

Dedicated: To my amazing Wife, director of all things good and wonderful.

Acknowledgements: I would like to thank everyone who has ever read a single page of the play from its conception on my MFA program to all the readings. First off, Tom Provost, Brian Asman, Christian Toumayan, and Sarah Sheppeck who livened up a scene. Next, the first act reading and full reading: Mike Detrow, Phillip Gabriel, Britney Gomez-Landeros, Damaris Vizvett, and Jason Crewse. Once again, these amazing people prove that love doesn't always bite, though it is sometimes sharp.

Characters:

MAN WHO NEVER MISSES: Representing an archer of famous reputation, whose name is a misnomer.

MIRICAL MAKER: A mage who is known for miraculous magic, though he forgot how to cast a spell outside of theory.

BARB KING: A former blacksmith who purchased the tower besieged by a dragon and containing a mysterious girl who he wishes to be his queen.

MYSTERIOUS FIGURE: A girl dressed in brown robes and cloaked. No one knows her purpose. She came with the tower.

DRAGON: Female, any age, dressed all in red. Must be strong and commanding representing a pissed off/horny dragon.

Playwrights note When speaking Latin for "magical" words, either look up or make it up as it sounds.

ACT I

Place: *A castle tower. Outside, a dragon roars, startling three of the four people inside the room. The fourth,* **MYSTERIOUS FIGURE***, remains stoic, wearing a simple brown robe and sitting on a block.* **MAN WHO NEVER MISSES** *paces from murder hole to murder hole, holding his unstrung bow, ignoring his quiver of arrows.* **MIRICAL MAKER** *leans on his staff, studying tarot cards laid out before him on the floor.* **BARB KING** *holds his sword, still in its scabbard, in his lap, covering his ears, rocking back and forth, and crying,* "We are going to die," "Crispy critters." "Our asses are ashes." *Etc...*

MAN WHO NEVER MISSES: I don't have a clear shot. Bugger keeps circling too fast.

MIRICAL MAKER: If I were a dragon, I wouldn't let you have a clear shot at me, either.

MAN WHO NEVER MISSES: If you were a dragon, then we wouldn't have to worry about that beast circling around us. You'd soar from these stonewalls, sun light shimmering off your scales as you engaged our nemesis. Huge bodies thumping together like lovers in the throes of passion, claws tearing into thick flesh. It'd be a glorious battle. Flames gushing, a fountain of pure sunlight, engulfing each other until you danced in a ring of fire, teeth tearing each other's throats, wings kicking up a whirlwind, a storm unlike anything mankind has ever seen. Then, the stones would crack at the mighty death throes, after you tore the bastard's heart out and tossed his carcass to the ground.

MIRICAL MAKER: I think you missed your calling.

MAN WHO NEVER MISSES: I never miss anything.

MIRICAL MAKER: Pity. You would have made an excellent bard. Except you *missed* an important detail in the story.

MAN WHO NEVER MISSES: What detail?

MIRICAL MAKER: If I were a dragon, I'd eat you all myself.

BARB KING: Your ceaseless prattle is eating my brains. Would you just shut up and do your duty. You, *points at MWNM,* stick an arrow in its craw. You, *points at MM*, have you divined anything of how the dragon dies? Or our own deaths?

MIRICAL MAKER: All this noise makes it hard to concentrate.

MAN WHO NEVER MISSES: I'll make sure to tell the dragon to quiet down so you can think.

MIRICAL MAKER: You have a better chance of hitting something by, you know, stringing your bow and aiming an arrow at it. You miss every shot you don't take.

MAN WHO NEVER MISSES: I don't tell you how to do your flibdibly-flabdibly and Ohhmmmn BLAM! So don't tell me how to do mine. It's not so easy pointing an arrow out a thin slit and hitting a moving target. Archery is all about precision. Gauging the wind speed. Holding the right tension, and try not to breathe until the arrow flies off. Then there's the beast's scales. A metal arrow head would bounce right off like mosquitoes trying to suck steel plate. I would need one clear shot at its underbelly. There, the beast's delicate soft parts hide by which I can pierce its heart and make it fall.

MIRICAL MAKER: Now you speak as though you want to woo it.

MAN WHO NEVER MISSES: I could do worse. Like your father when he bedded your mother.

MIRICAL MAKER: Ah! I see something.

BK and MWNM gather around the tarot cards.

MAN WHO NEVER MISSES: The dragon's death?

BARB KING: Our death?

MAN WHO NEVER MISSES: A glorious victory?

BARB KING: Melting flesh and bone?

MIRICAL MAKER: *to MWNM.* Your real father. He's a troll from the stinking shit swamps. I guess that's where you get your charming personality and good looks.

BARB KING: If the dragon don't kill us, you two will be the death of me.

MIRICAL MAKER: It's not our fault you wanted this tower in the middle of nowhere. I advised against it, but you had to have it.

BARB KING: A king without a castle isn't much of a king.

MAN WHO NEVER MISSES: Or subjects to rule.

MIRICAL MAKER: Or vassals to tax and conscript for your army.

MAN WHO NEVER MISSES: Look on the bright side, you do have a dragon.

MIRICAL MAKER: Not many kings can say they have one of those left.

MAN WHO NEVER MISSES: The smart, wise, powerful kings had their knights kill all the dragons within a hundred leagues of their castle walls. That way they couldn't be trapped behind their stone walls waiting for it to become a mausoleum.

BARB KING: I don't have knights. I only have you two. Oh gods, we're dragon chow.

MIRICAL MAKER: Might be better that way. A quick, easy, painless death… but then again, I never felt the jaws of a dragon crunch my bones. I can't imagine it would be a pleasant experience. Just one you would never forget. At this stage, good King of the, ahum, castle, we are exactly all you have. Three—

MAN WHO NEVER MISSES: A one man army isn't much of an army.

MIRICAL MAKER: One man? Who?

MAN WHO NEVER MISSES: The only one in this motley bunch who knows how to fight.

MIRICAL MAKER: She's over there, being oh so helpful.

MAN WHO NEVER MISSES: Oh, ho ho! I forgot she was there. I thought she was some statue. Like one of them gargoyles to ward of the evil spirits. Did she come with you? Is she your assistant? An apostle?

MIRICAL MAKER: Apprentice? I haven't had one of those since the... the incident. So, she didn't come here with you and I didn't bring her....

MAN WHO NEVER MISSES: Maybe she belongs to the dragon. *Addresses MF*. Excuse me, Miss. Where did you come from?

BARB KING: I already tried that. She won't respond.

MIRICAL MAKER: Catatonic?

MAN WHO NEVER MISSES: I prefer mine with gin. Shaken. Sans hairball.

BARB KING: When I first moved in, she was here. A silent immoveable force, one devout in listening and vigilance. I tossed my jacket on her thinking she was nothing more than some old furniture left over from the previous resident... Paid that bastard necromancer a small fortune, for the view, he says. All about location. Location. Location. Shut your trap door, mage, I don't want to hear you warned me. Never trust a man in a cloak when you can't see his face.

I had to clear out a few skeletons from the closets, you know, some odd ball body parts left lying around and wriggling. A few talking heads whined, 'Where's my master! I want Master! When's supper?' I dumped the creepy bastards into the dried-up moat. Too many mouths to feed, you know. Still, that didn't shut'em up. At night you can still hear them screaming like some banshee in heat. When I took my jacket, to go outside and stomp on them some, *motions to MF,* her hood fell down and I saw it was a woman. A woman all the ways out here. Lonely, except for them stupid, whining heads, terrible at holding down a conversation. Well, I spent all night trying to engage her, being all polite-like. I asked her the meaningful questions: her name, her parentage, and her breast sizes. We were hitting it off real swell: me talking and she just listening, nary a response. The perfect woman one might say. Then those heads start to curse me and my sons. More the fools they, since I ain't got children, nor ever will, thank the gods. Plenty of bastards to populate a kingdom, but none I pay a copper for.

MAN WHO NEVER MISSES: Children are expensive. Having to feed and keep them from drinking plague water. A complete drain of energy, I tell you.

BARB KING: The entire time her eyes stay fixed. She's like one of those paintings that no matter where you stand in the room, the eyes follow you. So, I start to pace and I swear her eyes are tracking me, but she shows no sign of life. They never blink once. I never had a woman so deeply entranced by me. I was her entire world filled up in those deep eyes, like she was seeing through me. Into my very soul.

MAN WHO NEVER MISSES: I get the see through you part. She's staring right past me.

BARB KING: I conclude she's under some sort of spell from the necromancer and he just forgot to take her with him. I mean, I could throw her out in the moat with the rest of the body parts, but she's, you know, too pretty, and... and such a great listener.

MAN WHO NEVER MISSES: What kind of monster leaves a perfectly good enchanted woman behind?

MIRICAL MAKER: The kind that brings dead people back to life to serve as slaves.

BARB KING: I covered her again, because those eyes, they are sort of creepy. They were reading too much into me, accusing me of being too solid, too much stone and bone, and not enough flesh. Who am I to ask for love? Who am I... A King...a King must not be soft, but hard as the metal he wishes forged. *To MM*. That's why I summoned you, before that fucking beast pinned us in here. To soften her up some. Bring this statue to life. In all this life and death struggle, I forgot about her.

MAN WHO NEVER MISSES: A dragon would do that. Who needs love when you might be shat out the tail end of a dragon at any moment?

BARB KING: What can you do, mage? Can you break her enchantment? Make her talk, at least? Would be nice to hear a woman's voice around this dump.

MIRICAL MAKER: I could...I mean, it shouldn't prove too difficult a spell to break. But I think you will be doing her a disservice. Hear me out before you object. Consider our circumstances. What are our odds of surviving this dragon? Ten to one.

MAN WHO NEVER MISSES: One hundred to one is my stake.

MIRICAL MAKER: The gods know the odds favor the dragon in this fight. Would it be a kindness to break her enchantment, essentially wake her up to either starve in this siege, or be roasted by dragon fire, dying a horrific death all the while knowing it was you and I to blame for her pain, her misery? Or let her remain as is, until some knight comes and kiss her to break the spell?

MAN WHO NEVER MISSES: Or fried unaware. Like pouring boiling water on a sleeping ant hill. Hush little ones, it'll soon be over.

BARB KING: A kiss will break the spell?

MIRICAL MAKER: Or turn you into a frog. Depends on the spell.

BARB KING: What are the odds of being turned into a frog?

MIRICAL MAKER: The same for being eaten by the dragon.

BARB KING: Not very good.

MAN WHO NEVER MISSES: I've always wondered what frog's legs tasted like.

BARB KING: You wouldn't.

MAN WHO NEVER MISSES: Why not? The dragon would eat you as a disgusting human. Why shouldn't I eat you as a frog?

BARB KING: Because I am your king and you're my subject. A subject is not supposed to eat his king.

MAN WHO NEVER MISSES: Technically we are hired help, not subjects.

MIRICAL MAKER: It is ill-advised to kiss a woman without their permission, regardless of their state of consciousness.

MAN WHO NEVER MISSES: You might taste better than the stagnant water and mealy-bugged oats.

BARB KING: Damitt! I am king and I can kiss who I want to kiss. And they will enjoy it, because I am a great kisser. *Leans in to kiss MWNM.*

MAN WHO NEVER MISSES: Whoa! Kiss him, not me. He said it.

BARB KING: Any other way, besides kissing the maiden, to break the enchantment?

MIRICAL MAKER: I'll have to consult the spirits.

MAN WHO NEVER MISSES: All out of those, too. I'd give a month's wages for a canter of good wine.

BARB KING: Whatever you have to do, do it. A king is a useless title without that extra something to make him a king.

MAN WHO NEVER MISSES: What would that extra something be?

BARB KING: A queen. If I am to die, I want to die a legitimate king, not some gilded imposter.

MIRICAL MAKER: How do you know she will consent to marriage?

BARB KING: She will. What woman wouldn't want to be a queen? Even if it's for a few hours. I don't have the gold or fine clothes, a jewel or a ring to place on her delicate fingers... but those are just material objects, easy to gain and just as easy to lose. The title, Queen, that isn't given to just anyone. It takes a special woman to wear the crown.

MAN WHO NEVER MISSES: But you don't have an extra crown.

BARB KING: She can have mine. All that I own will be hers, well, not legally, but in the spirit of the law, and through any male heirs she bears me. Assuming we live long enough to consummate the marriage. And yes, you heard me right, I would endure children for her. Their squealing, whining, puking, shitty and urine-stained nappies. I shall endure it all.

MIRICAL MAKER: The hopeless romantic. Make sure to use those exact words when you propose. 'You will be my queen and I will endure any children you squeeze out from between your loins.' That is sure to convince her.

MAN WHO NEVER MISSES: Oh yes, every peasant girl dreams of a place like this. A blank canvass she could paint with her feminine desires. A vase of flowers on the... the table, you need to get a table with chairs. Hang a painting of fruit there. A rug here. Curtains to cover up the view of a hungry dragon. If you don't see it, it doesn't exist. Many a good marriage is founded on that principle.

BARB KING: Then climb to the top of the tower and shoot that scaly, whoring fire-bird down.

MIRICAL MAKER: Phoenix is the fire bird, not a dragon. That would be a fire lizard.

MAN WHO NEVER MISSES: You want me. To go to. To. To. The top... of the tower... where I'll be exposed to fire and claws and...

Dragon roars and everyone, except MF, ducks.

teeth.

BARB KING: Yes! One shot and it's dead.

MAN WHO NEVER MISSES: Does it have to be an arrow? Couldn't it be a magical missile or some fireball the size of the sun?

MIRICAL MAKER: Don't be absurd. It's a fire elemental dragon. It would be like trying to douse a bonfire by tossing in a lit candle. Even if it were any other species of dragon, the power to create a fireball the size of the sun would be immense! Not that I couldn't do it, not that I couldn't do it. I choose not to! The drain on my personal health would be too great. I would be an invalid for a month. If summoning up such great power was easy, then every cheap conjuror of tricks would be doing it.

MAN WHO NEVER MISSES: I heard about the mage in the Prince Silver Locke's company. He brought an entire mountain down on a horde of trolls.
MIRICAL MAKER: You got the story mixed up.

MAN WHO NEVER MISSES: Are you sure? The way I heard it Prince Silver Locke's villages were harassed by the trolls. The hairy, ugly bastards kept stealing women and children to put in their cooking pots. So, the Prince leads his men and the mage in a desperate battle against the beasts. Just when everything was looking bleak, the mage holds his staff aloft and utters such powerful words. The earth shook and a great, big pile of stone crashes down and crushes every last one of the smelly bastards. Hundreds of lives were spared a hideous fate and the woman and children were released from the cooking fires.

BARB KING: Wish we had that mage here.

MIRICAL MAKER: You're wrong. Prince Silver Locke died, along with his men. The fool mage tried to open the earth up to swallow the entire horde, but instead created a fissure wide enough to drop the army into the trolls' stinking nests below.

MAN WHO NEVER MISSES: From the frying pan straight to the fire. I bet he used the passive tense in the spell, rather than the active verb. Tell me mage. What good is magic when you have a better chance of killing your friends than you do the enemy?

BARB KING: What use are you, Mage? You're not attacking the dragon or freeing the girl from the spell. Maybe we should stake you atop of the tower for bait and wait for the dragon to feast. As it grows fat on him, you and I attack it with bow and sword.

MIRICAL MAKER: Wait a moment... I haven't seen you draw the sword once. Do you even know how to use it? Or you, do you know how to string a bow?

MAN WHO NEVER MISSES: String a bow! I'm insulted.

BARB KING: *draws out his sword.* Want to find out?

MIRICAL MAKER: *holds staff defensively* Let's see if you know where the sharp end goes and if you get it there before I turn you to stone!

BARB KING: I'll stick you with the pointy end nice and slow.

MM tosses his hand out and mutters some incomprehensible words, like "Flash dancier" or "Moonlight sonata." A flash of white light and loud popping noises. BK and MWNM squeal and back away.

MAN WHO NEVER MISSES: You almost singed me!

BARB KING: Gods' damn, I wasn't going to hurt you?

MIRICAL MAKER: *waves staff at them.* Rigid Rict— *MWNM smacks MM with his bow—* Ow! What'd you do that for!

MAN WHO NEVER MISSES: I felt myself getting hard. You were turning us to stone!

BARB KING: I wasn't going to *really* feed you to the dragon. Trying to inspire you.

MIRICAL MAKER: Fear is a great motivator, but not when you threaten a mage!

Strikes MWNM with staff.

You don't hit one either. I'm not some dog.

MAN WHO NEVER MISSES: When you cast a spell on me, I do. Sit. Stay. Who's a good mage, who's a good mage.

MIRICAL MAKER: I wouldn't need to cast a spell on you, if I wasn't threatened with being made into dragon bait.

BARB KING: We just need to calm the fuck down.

MIRICAL MAKER: This coming from mister sword waver, 'wanna find out.' You found out alright.

BARB KING: Big man waving your stick around and muttering *homo erectus* to make us all hard. *Thrusts sword grip in MWNM's arms and raises fists.* You want to do this, let's do this, you tight-robed, dragon fucker.

MIRICAL MAKER: *Tosses staff to MWNM and strips off his robe to reveal a loin cloth.* Time to knock off the ugly and make your face pretty.

BK and MM start swinging at each other, knocking each other to the floor and rolling around. Swearing and cursing each other and their lineage. A loud roar from the dragon makes them stop and look at the murder holes.

MAN WHO NEVER MISSES: That was close. I could see his underbelly.

BARB KING: Why didn't you shoot it?

MAN WHO NEVER MISSES: My arms were kind of full. If you two are done wrestling and getting all sweaty on the floor, maybe we could figure out how to fight this dragon?

BK and MM look at each other.

BARB KING: I am, if he is.

MIRICAL MAKER: Fine.

Takes back the robe and puts it on.

It's really annoying how everyone thinks the mage can only fight using his words and staff. I was a professional wrestler in my younger days.

BARB KING: Explains the head lock.

MIRICAL MAKER: I am more than my words. You know how you say magic is worthless. It's because you don't understand it.

MAN WHO NEVER MISSES: Who really understands magic, anyway?

MIRICAL MAKER: Someone who has studied it for a millennium.

BARB KING: You don't look that old.

MAN WHO NEVER MISSES: A bit dusty, but not old. Alright, mister smarty-robes. Explain magic to us.

MIRICAL MAKER: Would be easier to help the dragon understand not to eat us.

BARB KING: So you can't give us the short version, a little watered down?

MIRICAL MAKER: There's not enough water in the entire ocean.
Do you really want to know?

Some shrugs and nods

> Fine. I will try to explain to you so your uneducated minds might catch a glimpse of how magic truly works.

It is a secret, and as with all secrets, I will need to swear you to secrecy. That you will never tell. On pain of watching your penis shrivel up like a worm caught on a hot rock, blacken and rot away, leaving a dark hole as a reminder of the promise you broke.

MAN WHO NEVER MISSES: Alright.

BARB KING: *sheathing sword*. Sure we got nothing better to do. I swear on my unshriveled penis not to tell a soul.

MIRICAL MAKER motions for them to sit down.

MIRICAL MAKER: Magic. Magic... alright Magic. Magic is explaining the explainable that is unexplainable due to our limited perceptions. The idea of defying the natural, making it unnatural. We experience the world through our senses. The picture goes to our brain, but somewhere it gets all distorted. Emotions color what we see and how we see it. When you get mad, the slightest comment, though harmless can seem a great jab—

BARB KING: Boring! Tell me something I don't know.

MAN WHO NEVER MISSES: Tell us about the smoke and mirrors, the prestidigitation.

BARB KING: The words. What are the magic words? *Homo erectus* or the *flash in the pan.*

MIRICAL MAKER: There isn't any magic words.

BARB KING: Dragon shit! What's all that goblin-guck that falls out of your mouth during those incantations?

MIRICAL MAKER: Gobbledygook? It's not about the words. It's about the meaning behind the words. Our intentions.

MAN WHO NEVER MISSES: Intentions. That's good. The same thing the marksman archer uses to hit the buckseye every time.

MIRICAL MAKER: Bullseye.

MAN WHO NEVER MISSES: Haven't hunted a bull, but I did once bring down a twelve point buck.

BARB KING: In season, otherwise it doesn't count.

MAN WHO NEVER MISSES: Of course in season.

BARB KING: What about a twelve-hundred-point dragon?

MAN WHO NEVER MISSES: That's trickier.

MIRICAL MAKER: Do you want to know about magic, or not?

BK and MWNM returns their attention back to MM

Magic is intentions. You have to feel it, become one with the flow of time and space. Once you feel it, you got to mean what you say and say what you mean. Any slight deviation and that mountain you wanted to crash down on your enemies, smashes you instead. Do you understand what I mean?

MAN WHO NEVER MISSES: No. Because you really didn't say anything about magic except to "feel" it and "mean" it. Also, not to fuck up the wording otherwise a mountain will crush you.

MIRICAL MAKER: Of course, you wouldn't understand. The very act of explaining magic, diminishes it. Like explaining a rainbow to a blind man.

BARB KING: Alright, mage. How would you feel out the destruction of this dragon? None of us is getting out of here until either the fiery bastard is dead or we're carried out in its belly.

MIRICAL MAKER: First, we have to understand what it wants.

MAN WHO NEVER MISSES: What it wants is to eat us.

MIRICAL MAKER: Yes, but why?

BARB KING: Because it's hungry.

MIRICAL MAKER: Hungry for what, exactly?

MAN WHO NEVER MISSES: Man flesh.

BARB KING: Roasted king.

MIRICAL MAKER: But you are not a king, according to your definitions. You don't have subjects, a wife, vassals to collect taxes from or an army to kill your dragon.

MAN WHO NEVER MISSES: He does have a crown.

MIRICAL MAKER: The hat doesn't make the man. Nor a crown a king makes.

BARB KING: What I have is a couple of jesters. What I need, oh wise mage, is not pontifications, but perforations in the dragon's scales. Were your magic as sharp as your wit, we'd be bathing in dragon's blood. So, give me something useful to kill the bastard.

MIRICAL MAKER: What do you think the dragon wants? When did it first show up?

BARB KING: Like a rotten neighbor home from vacation, this bastard reared its scaly head right after I moved into the place.

MAN WHO NEVER MISSES: So, you have to move. There are plenty more towers that don't come with pet dragons.

BARB KING: I don't want to. The value on this place has dropped and I won't recoup any of my investment.

MIRICAL MAKER: You could recoup your skin intact.

BARB KING: Come to think of it, the dragon didn't rear its scaly head until you both came. Who's to say one of you didn't bring the beast with you? Try to scare me away from my investment. Maybe you heard about buried treasure. Dragons love gold and jewels and anything that shines. I wouldn't doubt one of you made a deal with it. Chase out the old king so you can find the treasure.

MIRICAL MAKER: Now you are being foolish. Blaming the exterminator for letting the mice into the house.

MAN WHO NEVER MISSES: Did you ask the talking heads about treasure their master may have buried?

BARB KING: Why would I ask them? They won't even look at me.

MAN WHO NEVER MISSES: Especially now after you kicked them out to the moat.

BARB KING: *to MM*. Maybe you divined it from your cards. That's why you came so fast to help me with the girl. You wanted the treasure and the girl, for your own.

MAN WHO NEVER MISSES: Would make sense as to why he don't want to put a spell on the dragon.

BARB KING: Or he cast an illusion spell on us. To make us think the dragon is real when it could all be made up in our heads.

Dragon roars.

MAN WHO NEVER MISSES: He's good. It sounds so real.

MIRICAL MAKER: Maybe you both should go tell that to the dragon. See if his teeth and claws are an illusion.

MAN WHO NEVER MISSES: I think he is casting another spell on us. My head feels kind of fuzzy. I want to go out and see if the dragon is real. Which means it probably is and we are creating the illusion that it's not real. As soon as we put one foot onto the parapet... Chomp! No more king. No more archer. The treasure belongs to him and his dragon familiar.

BARB KING: Stop with the mind tricks, mage!

MIRICAL MAKER: You have it all wrong. You are not supposed to deduce my intentions, which at this moment are to survive your stupidity, and the dragon.

No, you slugs! Ask what the dragon wants. Treasure, maybe. A quiet neighborhood without kings, also very likely. To eat. We are easy game. None of those feel like the answer.

BARB KING: Here we go again with feelings. I'm beginning to regret not tossing you to the dragon.

MIRICAL MAKER: What if you're wrong? Who'll wake the girl to be your queen? Or slay the dragon?

MAN WHO NEVER MISSES: He has a point. We need to work together to slay the bloody beast, but only he has the secret to wake the girl.

MIRICAL MAKER: Weigh your actions carefully. Fictional treasure.

MAN WHO NEVER MISSES: Or fictional magic.

BARB KING: Wake the girl.

MIRICAL MAKER: What about—

BARB KING: Wake the damn girl.

MIRICAL MAKER: No.

BARB KING: No.

MIRICAL MAKER: The girl is safe from the dragon. And you.

BARB KING: Dragon shit! I paid you to do a job, so wake her up.

MIRICAL MAKER: I can't

BARB KING: Can't or won't?

MIRICAL MAKER: Can't. Won't. All the same.

BARB KING: I know you know how. You are the most powerful mage this side of the fallen mountains. Wake her.

MIRICAL MAKER: You have yet to give me a single coin.

MAN WHO NEVER MISSES: Or me, for that matter. I don't do this kind of thing for credit or exposure. I have been exposed enough.

BARB KING: Neither of you gets paid until the dragon is dead and the girl woken.

MAN WHO NEVER MISSES: Wakened. Isn't it wakened?

MIRICAL MAKERR: Just keep quiet and sit over there. Perhaps string your bow incase the dragon decides to stop the fly-bys and enter the tower.

MAN WHO NEVER MISSES: Can it do that?

MIRICAL MAKER: *To BK.* As for you and your demands. I might just walk out of here and leave you with him to figure out both your problems. Unless you give me a gods-damned moment of peace so I can read my cards on how to solve the conundrum, I will leave.

BARB KING: You have until twilight. After that, you will do your mage thing and get us all out of here.

MIRICAL MAKER: I can't take all three of us. I didn't bring my cloak of invisibility.

BARB KING: I'm sure we can find another way for you to be useful.

MIRICAL MAKER shuffles tarot cards and begins to lay them out one by one. MAN WHO NEVER MISSES struggles to string his bow. A big show of him bending the bow and it snapping away, smacking various body parts in a slap-stick comedy. At one point leading him to strangle it like fighting a vicious creature until the string slips over the end and he holds it out victoriously, as though he has won a major battle. Tentatively he tests the bow in fear of the string snapping back and taking out an eye.

BARB KING takes center stage. He talks to the audience.

BARB KING: I will not bend to this dragon's fire.
I am the iron to strike it down.
Some boys grow up dreaming of being a brave
warrior. The shinning metal armor, sharp
weapons and a chance to fight and kill an enemy
for king and kingdom. The warrior takes on all
challenges, no matter the cost of the outcome. All
glory goes to the victor. Women. Food. Drink.
Riches taken by the living.
Weeping and wailing for the dead. Musty, cold
dirt, a final bed to sleep. Stone pillow. A feast for
worms. Songs sung, until you are forgotten or
replaced by another. No one ever remembers the
dead. It is the living who gain glory.
Fuck being a warrior. I became a king, instead.
Food. Drink. Woman. Riches to follow the gilded
crown. A bastard already sat on the throne and I
wasn't anything more than a son of a blacksmith,
valued because of my knowledge to make
weapons, not use them. To create works of art
from black sludge drudged up from the earth and
smelted down to something useful: a plow, a
shovel, an ax, a sword. I sold weapons to the
warriors. When they broke, I sold more. Until I
stocked up enough gold to buy a tower far away
from my country. A place without a king. A wild
place requiring the firm hand of divine rule. Inside
our frail flesh we are all divine, or at least we think
we are. Then the demon comes to challenge our
immortal soul. We discover how weak we really

are. A divine king requires no one, but himself to rule. An earthly king relies on others.

I am a simple man with an iron crown forged over his fire. Painted gold. Scratch the surface and a man's worth is shown. I am a cracked shell waiting to bleed. When I do bleed, it will be iron, not gold. Gold is soft, malleable too easy to fit any form. Iron must be struck over and over again with a hammer. Shaped by fire and force.

I am the hammer and this is my forge.

BK draws his sword and prepares to exit.

MAN WHO NEVER MISSES: Where are you going?

BARB KING: To challenge the dragon to a one-on-one fight.

MAN WHO NEVER MISSES: That thing is like ten of you. The dragon would have to agree to be muzzled, blind folded, wings clipped, claws trimmed and it could still roll over and crush you.

BARB KING: I am tired of cowards ignoring my commands, too afraid to face the beast. Let the gods decide my fate.

MAN WHO NEVER MISSES: But he's not done divining our plan from the cards. At least let him finish with the cards before you walk to certain death. I mean, you are not a king, really. Wait a bit longer. I will swear my fealty to you so you have

29

one subject to bow before your grace. We can go
out together. Let us wait for the cards.

BARB KING: You will kneel to me?

MAN WHO NEVER MISSES: Both knees.

BARB KING: *sheaths sword*. I will be patient.

MAN WHO NEVER MISSES: You won't regret it.
I hope I don't.

MIRICAL MAKER: *Staring at cards*. Oh, ugh, ewww,
yuck, hmmmm. Yes. That's it!

BARB KING: Finally, an answer!

MAN WHO NEVER MISSES: What does it say?

MIRICAL MAKER: We have to wait.

BARB KING: Wait! For what?

MAN WHO NEVER MISSES: The dragon will get
bored and leave us alone?

BARB KING: Tell me it's a champion knight-errant
come to slay it.

MIRICAL MAKER: We are waiting. For something else.

BARB KING: What the hell else are we waiting for? The
dragon to figure out we are three beans in a can

ready to heat up. For him to figure out which way the arrow goes on the bow? For you conjure more cheap magic tricks, to stall me from getting what I want. All I want—

MAN WHO NEVER MISSES: For us to kill the fucking dragon and him to wake your bride to be.

BARB KING: I'm tired of waiting. Since you won't let me fight the dragon—

BK pushes the hood back on MF and kisses her. MM and MWNM gasp. Dragon roars. BK steps back waiting for something to happen. Nothing happens.

MAN WHO NEVER MISSES: How do you feel?

BARB KING: The same.

MIRICAL MAKER: No tingling in the extremities.

BARB KING: Nothing beyond the usual tingling when I kiss a woman.

MAN WHO NEVER MISSES: How long before he turns into a frog?

MIRICAL MAKER: By now, he would have looked mighty green, grown webbed toes, and acquired an appetite for flies.

MAN WHO NEVER MISSES: Are you hungry for flies?

BK shakes his head

How disappointing.

BARB KING: I'll never be a king. I'll die a lonely peasant in my tower of stone.

MYSTERIOUS FIGURE: Not the best kiss I ever had.

The three men turn in shock. MF has her hood down and is stretching, as though waking from a long nap.

Why are you all gawping at me? Haven't you ever seen a woman before?

MIRICAL MAKER: It worked.

BARB KING: You sound so surprised.

MIRICAL MAKER: I mean. This is what the cards told me. It's all about intentions. Had you kissed her without the feeling of desperation, she wouldn't have turned—

BARB KING/MYSTERIOUS FIGURE: Dragon shit!

MAN WHO NEVER MISSES: It's a miracle!

BARB KING: Who are you?

MYSTERIOUS FIGURE: Who are you?

BARB KING: I am king of this tower.

MYSTERIOUS FIGURE: Oh, so you don't—

BARB KING: Don't what?

MYSTERIOUS FIGURE: Know what happened to Bernard?

MAN WHO NEVER MISSES: Bernard?

MIRICAL MAKER: The necromancer who owned it before.

MYSTERIOUS FIGURE: His name is Bernard. Did you kill him? I guess it would be ironic if you did. He was always playing with dead things. Bringing them back to half-life.

MAN WHO NEVER MISSES: Half-life?

MIRICAL MAKER: Once something is dead it cannot be brought all the back to this side of the life. Not without consequences.

BARB KING: I bought this place from him.

MYSTERIOUS FIGURE: Where are his brothers?

BARB KING: He was alone when I bought it.

MYSTERIOUS FIGURE: They would have been only heads. A run in with a dragon singed their bodies into lumps of coal. But their heads were left intact and they screamed and wailed until they began to die. Bernard brought them back to half-alive.

MAN WHO NEVER MISSES: They are in the—*BK kicks him*—Ow!

BARB KING: He must've taken them when he left.

MYSTERIOUS FIGURE: Oh. Do you know where he went?

BARB KING: He didn't say.

Dragon roars again.

MYSTERIOUS FIGURE: That thing is still around? Now you know why he sold the place.

BARB KING: I wish he'd disclosed the dragon before I bought this lovely piece of real estate.

MYSTERIOUS FIGURE: It's his fault the dragon is here.

MIRICAL MAKER: See. It wasn't me.

MAN WHO NEVER MISSES: What did he do? Steal an egg?

MYSTERIOUS FIGURE: ....

MIRICAL MAKER: Seven hells, he didn't!

MYSTERIOUS FIGURE: Said he needed it for an experiment.

MIRICAL MAKER: Gods! We are dead.

BARB KING: Couldn't we just give it back?

MYSTERIOUS FIGURE: It broke...on accident.

MIRICAL MAKER: He broke the fucking thing! How did he break a dragon's egg? The shell is thicker than these stone walls.

MAN WHO NEVER MISSES: That sounds bad. All bad. Like bend me over a post and let a horse bugger me bad.

MYSTERIOUS FIGURE: Only it won't be a horse, but a dragon.

MAN WHO NEVER MISSES: All the more exciting.

BARB KING: No wonder he was in a hurry to leave.

MAN WHO NEVER MISSES: What I don't get is why this Bernard would leave you behind? Was he your husband? *MF shakes head at each.* Boyfriend? Friend with benefits?

MYSTERIOUS FIGURE: I was his beastologist.

MAN WHO NEVER MISSES: No wonder he left you. Some fetishes I understand—

MIRICAL MAKER: Beastologist, you idiot, not bestiality. He hired you to figure out how to get rid of the dragon.

MYSTERIOUS FIGURE: Exactly.

BARB KING: So you know how?

MYSTERIOUS FIGURE: Not exactly.

BARB KING: No wonder he turned you into a statue. You were more useful as my coat hanger. *MF begins to cry.* Er, I mean, you were, are, so very lovely, and I'm certain we can solve this issue together. How would you like to be—

MIRICAL MAKER: My assistant. I could use any knowledge you've gained.

MYSTERIOUS FIGURE: Who are you?

MIRICAL MAKER: A humble mage trying to save us from the dragon.

MYSTERIOUS FIGURE: Yes, that would be nice. To help out a humble mage.

They go off to the side, conversing about Dragonology.

BARB KING: *to MWNM.* What's he doing? She's supposed to be my queen, not his personal assistant. Do you think he is trying to win her over? To steal away my chance at happiness? My opportunity to solidify my kingliness? What? Why aren't you responding?

MAN WHO NEVER MISSES: Because you won't let me.

BARB KING: Speak now.

MAN WHO NEVER MISSES: I think he saved you from a social blunder. You insulted her worth and compared her to a coat rack. Those are not the most endearing words when trying to woo a woman. Might I suggest you compliment her on something other than her beauty and ability to hold coats?

BARB KING: Very wise words. I will take your counsel and speak to her now, before that mage ruins her with his words. I know a spell or two to win the hearts of the ladies.

BK moves to MF and listens to the silent conversation, leaving MWNM alone at center stage.

MAN WHO NEVER MISSES: The first time I picked up a bow I was eight years old. It was winter and the harvest wasn't a good one. We were down to eating the last of the weevils in the grain. My father gave me the bow and three arrows, since in the war he took a mace to his head, crushing an eye socket and he could no longer see well-enough to shoot. We had to make every shot count. Missing meant one of us would go hungry that night. It wouldn't be him, he assured me. We came upon a deer trail. Tracked it until midday, my toes freezing in my boots soaked through by the snow. My fingers were thick wooden blocks when we saw the first one, a long-legged doe, nibbling on evergreen bark. My father had me crouch. He handed me the first arrow and showed me how to nock it so it wouldn't fall off the string or shoot myself in the foot. Icicle fingers drew the taut string back, feather tickling frost bloomed cheek. The doe stood at the end of the steel tip, her white breast open to me. I could almost hear her heart beat. The warm blood pulsing in her veins. I held my breath, then let it out in a cold puff. The arrow leapt from my hands and pierced her heart. For an instant, her large brown eyes met mine. She asked me if I was death and what would become of her children? Droplets of blood dripped into the white snow. Her legs became heavy and she stumbled, her eyes locked on mine, waiting for an answer. I will kill them, too, I told her.

That was a lie. I never found her children, or had a father nearly blinded by a mace, or touched a bow until my journey to this tower. That story belonged to my cousin and I borrowed it to pay off a debt to a king.

In reality, I'm a simple man. A drunkard who killed a man in a brawl. A man who was the favorite bed fellow to the king. Instead of striking me dead, he gave me a choice. A life for a life. I must execute a rival or else my cousin will die because of my stupid actions.

Except, I never killed a man before. Lost every fight I was a part of. The king's fop slipped on some spilled ale and smashed his head on the bar, his brains leaking out like spoiled eggs. Since I was the closest to him at the bar when he died, I was blamed and my cousin imprisoned.

So I must play my part. Another innocent must die in place of my cousin. I must do what I've never done before. To use hands more suited to lifting a mug now to nock an arrow on a bow I never used to kill a man I never knew and free a man I never was.

Might be easier if the dragon ate us all, if not for the fact I need to bring this tin king's head back in a bag to free my cousin.

I must kill the beast to protect the one I'm supposed to kill.

Life was easier swimming in a mug.

MF smacks BK. BK stumbles back to MWNM.

What happened?

BARB KING: I did what you said. I told her she had a nice ass.

MAN WHO NEVER MISSES: I didn't tell you to be an ass. When you talk to a woman, treat her like a person, rather than an object. Talk about her wit and charm. For god's sake, don't ask her to be your queen!

BARB KING: Why not? That's the whole point of the conversation.

MAN WHO NEVER MISSES: You don't need to so blunt. She isn't a nail you need to hammer. You can't shape her into something she doesn't want to be. That's a woman's job to shape us men. You need to court her.

BARB KING: I don't have time to go pick her flowers or wine and dine her, not with that dragon trying to wine and dine on us.

MAN WHO NEVER MISSES: Then you'll never win her heart.

BARB KING: I don't need her heart, just her vows.

MAN WHO NEVER MISSES: Words are empty unless they have the heart to fill them up.

BARB KING: When we have the dragon's heart, I will be sure to give it to her.

MAN WHO NEVER MISSES: I would say give her yours, but you haven't got one.

BARB KING: Who needs a heart when his sword is long?

MAN WHO NEVER MISSES: Not as long as others.

BARB KING: It's all in the skill of using it.

MAN WHO NEVER MISSES: I've never played with swords, so I wouldn't know how. But, I know a thing or three about a woman. I was married once. We were young and drunk on wildflower wine, playing in our fields. She was the rustic maid, not too thin, or too thick, freckles dotting her face enough to envy the stars in the sky and she had a laugh to light up the meadows. I tell you, happiness can be found nowhere if it can't be seen in the eyes of your lover.

BARB KING: What happened to her?

MAN WHO NEVER MISSES: She died.

BARB KING: Oh, I never heard this tale about the greatest marksmen in twelve kingdoms.

MAN WHO NEVER MISSES: Thirteen, once we win yours back from the dragon. No, it is a sad tale I don't tell. Because I lost both wife and child in one swipe of the butcher's knife. The babe was to be a boy, and he clung too long to his mother. I don't blame him. I would like to have rode to death with her. All I have left are the dreams at the bottom of empty mugs. Oh, and a cousin.

BARB KING: You say cousin like death hoovers over his shoulder.

MAN WHO NEVER MISSES: Very true words. He's imprisoned by a King Sampson.

BARB KING: Sampson is an ass. A ninny who spends more time wiping his noise on his sleeve, crying because someone spoiled his daughter.

MAN WHO NEVER MISSES: Did they?

BARB KING: It was me. The wench was double blessed with two bastards in her belly, last I saw her. Before I made my purchase of this cursed tower. King Sampson in a pushover. I will help you rescue this cousin of yours once we kill this dragon.

MAN WHO NEVER MISSES: I believe you. I will do everything in my power to hold you to your word.

MIRICAL MAKER: Well, I have good news and bad news.

BARB KING: Best to hear the bad news first and get it over.

MIRICAL MAKER: I had hoped the dragon would get bored, or hungry, and leave us eventually. But that isn't the case. Not since the necromancer took her egg and broke it. Her desire for retribution is too strong.

MAN WHO NEVER MISSES: Like pissing on a hornets nest. We are about to get stung in so many places.

BARB KING: What's the good news?

MYSTERIOUS FIGURE: *to MWNM* You have no idea how truly accurate is your analogy. One of you are going to have to woo the dragon.

BK/MWNM: What in the seven hells!/ How in the hells do you woo a dragon?

MYSTERIOUS FIGURE: You see, once her egg was stolen, she had to get it back. Dragon's only lay an egg once every twenty-five years or so. Since it was destroyed, well, her maternal instinct changed, drawn in by the strong musk this tower holds. To put it one way, she is a horny dragon.

MAN WHO NEVER MISSES: I saw claws on her, but not a single horn.

BARB KING: No, you idiot. What's he saying is one of us has to fuck a dragon.

MAN WHO NEVER MISSES: You wanted a queen, there's your chance.

BARB KING: How does this even work? I mean does she roll over and we climb on top of her? Or do we lay down and hope she doesn't fuck us into the ground?

MIRICAL MAKER: Neither. You go out there and try to mount her and she'll bite your head off.

MYSTERIOUS FIGURE: Bloody hell, where did you get your manners from? You can't just grab her like some common sheep and rut into her. You have to treat her like a lady. Didn't your mother teach you any better?

BARB KING: My mother was kidnapped from her town by my father and held prisoner until she consented to marry him.

MAN WHO NEVER MISSESS: Explains where you got your charms.

BARB KING: Seven hells! I guess I don't have the charm to woo a dragon. Which one of you two will it be?

MAN WHO NEVER MISSES: Ummm....

MIRICAL MAKER: Errr....

BARB KING: One of you has got to be better at charming a lady than you do at killing this dragon,

I mean you, *pointing at MWNM,* you told me how I have to win hearts and not with words, well, now's your chance to show me. Show me how great a marksman you truly are with the arrow of love.

MAN WHO NEVER MISSES: Whoah! I told you that story in confidence and, besides, I swore never to love again.

BARB KING: You only have to make her believe you love her, then you can dig into her scales.

MYSTERIOUS FIGURE: You are a wretched man. That's not at all how it will work. She will sense any falsehood and deception. Dragons are way smarter than you men. You have to truly mean it.

MAN WHO NEVER MISSES: Could you cast a love spell on the dragon? Make it believe she's in love with one of us?

MIRICAL MAKER: That would fall under the category of deception. Mind spells wouldn't work on a dragon anyway. They don't think like us.

MYSTERIOIS FIGURE: Much how men and women think differently.

BARB KING: Don't try logic on her, then.

MAN WHO NEVER MISSES: Love really isn't logical. It's more of a state-of-being.

BARB KING: *to MM* Have you ever been in love?

MIRICAL MAKER: Not that I recall, I mean, I am always open to it.

BARB KING: That leaves you, Marksmen. You are the only one here who has experienced love.

MYSTERIOUS FIGURE: I have been in love.

BARB KING: But you lack the essential sword for this mission.

MAN WHO NEVER MISSES: How is it even possible? Aren't we different species? I think this falls under the category of bestiality and not your bestiary, or whatever you call it. We don't speak the same language!

Dragon roars.

BARB KING: The language of love is universal. Sweet talk her, only in dragon.

MAN WHO NEVER MISSES: Roar. Roar. Gush flame. I don't think I have the lungs for that.

MYSTERIOUS FIGURE: A male dragon typically approaches the female dragon from behind, catching her when her back is arched. Then he uses his claws to hold on while she thrashes around trying to bite his head off. Oftentimes, after he fertilizes her egg, she catches him in his final ecstatic throes, severs his throat and feasts on his dead body, continuing to feed while she warms the egg, waiting for her hatchling to emerge, which takes up to a year. A great symbiotic relationship and keeps a population balanced. It's just a theory I formed from watching lizards mate.

MIRICAL MAKER: I like that theory.

MAN WHO NEVER MISSES: Can't we just kill her?

BARB KING: That's what I've been trying to get you two to do for the last day and a half, but I like the sound of this plan better.

MAN WHO NEVER MISSES: How will I know where to, um, sheath my sword?

MIRICAL MAKER: You will know.

MYSTERIOUS FIGURE: I am going to prepare a blend of aromatics to help draw her attention to the possible mating. What I need from you is your small clothes.

MAN WHO NEVER MISSES: I think I shat them. What do you need them for?

MYSTERIOUS FIGURE: So she can get your scent.

MAN WHO NEVER MISSES: Alright.

Removes pants and strips off underwear. Hands them to MF who shies away, pinching them between her fingers.

> Do you think I can get those back? They're my only pair.

MYSTERIOUS FIGURE: Um, no.

MF begins gathering items from her bag.

MAN WHO NEVER MISSES: What if this doesn't work? What if she doesn't like me or want me?

MIRICAL MAKER: Did you have cold feet on the eve of your wedding?

MAN WHO NEVER MISSES: No, I made sure to pack my boots with warm stockings before I left the village. I tried to run away, but her father and brothers caught up to me before I got a few yards from the gate. I showed up at the binding in my cleanest tunic and sporting a few bruises.

MIRICAL MAKER: After you mate with the dragon, a few bruises will be a good night for you.

BARB KING: Hells, you didn't have fun unless you got some kind of markings. Nails, teeth, fists, all make for a great night's romping. You do this right and appease the dragon's hunger, then I'll grant you any boon you want.

MAN WHO NEVER MISSES: You'll honor your word and help me free my cousin?

BARB KING: To put another one over that rat bastard Simon, I'll do that without your need to fuck a dragon.

MAN WHO NEVER MISSES: That's all I want. If I do this and the dragon goes away, you'll do everything within your power to free my cousin.

BARB KING: I swear by the gods above and devils below, on my word as a king, I will do everything in my power to help you free your cousin.

Spits on his palm and offers MWNM the hand. They shake.

MAN WHO NEVER MISSES: Done.

MF holds up soaked underwear

MYSTERIOUS FIGURE: Alright, I think this should work.

BARB KING: What's that awful smell?

MYSTERIOUS FIGURE: Dragon urine, skunk weed extract, and, *points to MWNM,* him.

MIRICAL MAKER: *At a murder hole*. Hurry, she's circling around again.

MF takes the underwear and tosses it out the murder hole.
They gather around, each trying to watch. Dragon roar, loud thud, loud sniffing and various other noises.

MAN WHO NEVER MISSES: What's she doing?

MIRICAL MAKER: Rolling on it.

MYSTERIOUS FIGURE: Getting his scent. This is a good sign.

BARB KING: What would be a bad sign?

MYSTERIOUS FIGURE: Burning it.

MAN WHO NEVER MISSES: Ew... is she—

MIRICAL MAKER: Eating them.

BARB KING: That a good sign?

MYSTERIOUS FIGURE: Very good sign.

BARB KING: *slapping MWNM on the back*. Looks like you are about to get lucky.

Flapping wings sound.

MAN WHO NEVER MISSES: Wait! Where is she going?

MYSTERIOUS FIGURE: To come meet you.

MAN WHO NEVER MISSES: What do you mean?

DRAGON enters. A woman dressed in red cloak, pants and tunic. She stops, looks each of them over and sniffs the air.

BARB KING: Who are you and what are you doing in my tower?

MAN WHO NEVER MISSES: How'd you get in here with the dragon outside?

MYSTERIOUS FIGURE: She's the dragon.

Lights out.

End Act 1.

Act 2

Spotlight of MM alone on the stage

MIRICAL MAKER: I fucked up. Not one of those little ones where you can shrug it off and go about your daily business as usual, but a giant hill of a fuck up. A mountain-sized fuck up, one might say. One moment you are cheered: "You're doing some great work, Mirical man!" and "Bring the wrath of God, Mirical." All smiles and laughter, pats on the back, a real ego boost that quickly turns into horrific screams echoing through the valley. When facing impossible odds with impeccable arts, one might have improbable expectations. Survival calls for extreme measures. Not much exceeds the gut-wrenching terror thousands of trolls creates when their thunderous feet cause the very earth to tremble beneath you. Twice the size of any man bore down upon us, clubs and swords and menacing weapons to smash, bash, and cleave a man in twain. It was a sight to cause grown men to weep and piss their pants, crying out for their mommies. Only fools and madmen lack fear. It is the brave who embrace the fear and stand their ground. I couldn't fail those brave men or their families. I hadn't, yet. They turned to me for salvation. Salvation. Like I was a god. God of Miracles. Performed enough that even I believed in my divinity.

That moment was no different. I stood in the center of the men, believing I could call down the walls of the valley on the trolls' heads. I knew the spell, memorized the wording and careful pronunciation. Always so careful with magic, because a single slip and...

That's when I fucked up. A moment of doubt crept in and I wondered what would happen if I failed those men. Then it happened. The stone floor swept away from under our feet. All around me were broken bodies, men with whom I shared a mug of bitter ale just the night before... before they became clam shells shattered on the rocks, pink flesh torn open in useless armor. Men moaned, cried, some calling for their mothers. Those who survived the fall scrambled around for swords, spears, anything to fend off the claws and teeth. Scaled-trolls tore into them, muzzles covered in grizzle and dripping gore. They smelled like soggy dogs matted with shit. There were too many and we were in their den, fallen in the proverbial soup pots. The trolls rendered the men limb-from-limb, decapitating and drinking their blood out of their skulls.

I watched. My eyes saturated by the horror. Magical words floated in my head, trapped by fear and guilt. I had caused this. I had switched the tense of the verbs. My dumb mouth so practiced in magic, mastering it by the age of eighteen, leading these men into the gapping maw of death. I spoke one more word of magic. Ignis. Fire. A simple word, one every novice masters first, but one when driven by the focused intensity caused by fear, it is the most destructive. The fire came, lighting the cavern up in a huge fucking firestorm. I burned men and troll alike. We were already dead, pieces of meat to fill the gawping maws of the beasts, and I had one duty. End it all.

I would have died in the fire, should have died, except whatever cruel god laughs from his high-mountain throne, had one last trick left. The intensity of my intentions blew a hole beneath me, and I plunged down into the deep cold water. I was swept away by an underground spring, carried to a far-off land. Words of magic forgotten, or maybe barricaded behind a wall of shame and guilt.

I wandered unknown towns and villages, falling into obscurity, living off simple illusions, pretending to do magic, to amaze the ignorant with great miracles. Truly, I performed the greatest of all miracles and disappeared.

Until fate found me facing down a dragon.

Snaps fingers and says "Ignis."

Lights up on the stage. MF, MWNM, BK frozen on the stage. MM takes his place next to MF and thumps his staff on the floor.

MAN WHO NEVER MISSES: She's a what?

DRAGON: Dragon. Don't tell me you are stupid. I can't mate with an imbecile. Think of the children.

MAN WHO NEVER MISSES: I think I just shat myself, again.

BARB KING: It's a wonder you ever married.

MYSTERIOUS FIGURE: Excuse us a moment. *Takes MWNM aside.* Eating the excrement of a potential mate may be acceptable among rabbits and dung beetles, but I assure you that is not a way to the heart of the dragon.

MIRICAL MAKER: Not very charming to talk about your bathroom habits until the third date at the very least.

MAN WHO NEVER MISSES: Is it hot in here or is it just me.

BARB KING: *motioning to the dragon.* It definitely got hot in here.

MAN WHO NEVER MISSES: You say she's like any other woman, right?

MIRICAL MAKER: One who will eat you if don't satisfy her needs.

MAN WHO NEVER MISSES: So, like any other woman.

MYSTERIOUS FIGURE: Because you smell like ass, doesn't mean you have to act like one.

MAN WHO NEVER MISSES: My apologies. I'm a bit nervous and scared and I say the wrong things... *To MM.* Can you make flowers and chocolate appear?

BARB KING: What the hell would a dragon do with flowers? Put it in a vase next to the pile of bones in her lair? She's here for one thing and one thing only. Put your big boy trousers on, drop those drawers, and mount that beast!

MYSTERIOUS FIGURE: Very charming. *To MWNM*. Keep in mind every species has their mating ritual. Frogs serenade with long, loud, and complex vocalizations that the lady frogs swoon over. Weaver birds build impressive nests. Some males have extravagant colors and others dance, strutting around until the girl chooses a partner. You have to go with your strength.

MAN WHO NEVER MISSES: I'm not much of a dancer, but get a few mugs of ale in me and I can sing the entire Dead Bards Saga. I can't promise it will be good.

BARB KING: I think I would rather be roasted than listen to you sing.

MYSTERIOUS FIGURE: Dragons covet three things. First is treasure. Second is strength. And the third is intelligence.

MAN WHO NEVER MISSES: The only gold I have is my tongue.

BARB KING: A good plan. Bore her to sleep with your stories and then you can fertilize her eggs.

MYSTERIOUS FIGURE: Remember, she will know if you are trying to deceive her. There's no telling how she will react if you tell a lie.

MIRICAL MAKER: I don't think it'll mean you'll be sleeping on the couch. Here, take my pouch. It has a few gold crowns.

BARB KING: Wear my crown. Royalty always impresses a lady.

MYSTERIOUS FIGURE: Put this around your neck. *hands MWNM a necklace.* It should help with your appeal.

MAN WHO NEVER MISSES: Smells like someone pissed on an onion.

MYSTERIOUS FIGURE: Dragon musk. Drives all the scaled-ladies crazy.

DRAGON: I grow bored. Bored and hungry.

MAN WHO NEVER MISSES: My lady beckons.

MWNM struts to DRAGON spits into his hand and slicks his hair back, sucks in his belly and puffs out his chest. Presents his leg in an embellished courtly bow.

What beauty do I see before me?

DRAGON: One who made you shit yourself, worm.

MAN WHO NEVER MISSES: That is just an expression where I come from. A woman of such beauty she makes you shit your pants. It's another way of saying you're weak in the knees, except you make my bowels watery.

DRAGON: I don't think it's my beauty that inspires your bowels.

Sniffs the air and licks her lips like she is about to eat a tasty meal.

What is that other smell? You smell delicious. I could eat you up.

Steps closer to MWHNM and he takes a step back, a strange sort of choreography where she approaches him and he counters.

BARB KING: You are not supposed to play hard to get.

MYSTERIOUS FIGURE: Hush, it's part of the mating ritual.

BARB KING: Looks like she's leading this dance.

MIRICAL MAKER: Stand your ground, man. Don't let her push you about. Strength. You have to show strength.

MAN WHO NEVER MISSES: Can we have a bit of wine before you, um, eat me up?

DRAGON: Why are you squirming, worm? Are you afraid of a little nip?

Snaps teeth.

MAN WHO NEVER MISSES: Depends on what you nip. I like my parts where they are, thank you very much. I mean, you are lovely, but I'm a moonlight walk on the beach kind-of-guy. Holding hands and listening to the sound of the waves.

DRAGON: The beach? Why? I hate the beach. Too much sand. It gets into everything. Between my toes, the folds of my wings, various cracks and crevices, no matter if you set blanket made of human skin down, the sand finds a way to stick to your scales. The ocean... don't get me started on fire and water. Give me the clear blue skies above the mountains, open grass lands to swoop down on yummy sheep and, on a good day, the shepherd. It's like eating clouds.

MAN WHO NEVER MISSES: I'm not so sure about the shepherd, but I do enjoy a nice roasted lamb chop.

DRAGON: You must try shepherd pie.

MAN WHO NEVER MISSES: I will keep that in mind next time I find myself out to pasture.

DRAGON: You stone dwellers are all the same. Hiding behind stone walls, afraid to stretch your wings and get wild.

MAN WHO NEVER MISSES: Going wild usually ends in two things. Death or a bad hangover. But hold on, I can be wild. The wildest of the bunch. I once rode a horse without a saddle. Or was it a saddle without a horse, I can't seem to get that story right. Anyway, I was married and the way I won her heart was through a drinking match. The man who was courting her at the time was a big guy, kind of dumb, like him. *Points to BK.*

BARB KING: Hey! That's an unfair stereotype. Not all big guys are dumb and not all little guys are clever. I happen to both.

MAN WHO NEVER MISSES: Clever and dumb. Anyway, back to my story. The man was eyeing up my Maggie. She was the prettiest girl in all the village not yet knocked up. So, he challenged me to a wrestling contest and rather than lose, I made him turn it into a drinking contest. I set up two kegs, one full of the darkest ale, and the other half-ale, half-water. Then we set to drinking. After ten cups he was piss drunk and vomited on Maggie, while I was only part drunk, which part I forget, but not drunk enough to forget I had won. I was the winner and she the most precious—

DRAGON: So, you cheated.

MAN WHO NEVER MISSES: Well, kind of. I may have won, but it was Maggie who lost. She died giving birth to my child, a son, who also died.

DRAGON: You know what it's like to lose a child. I was sitting on my egg when a strange dream came over me. I dreamt that a shadow crept into my cave and threatened to turn my unborn babe into a wraith unless I gave my egg to the shadow. The shadow promised no harm would come to my baby. In my dream I gave it my egg. Only, when I woke up, my egg was gone for real. The owner of this tower stole my baby. Worse, the shadow broke its promise. I found pieces of the shell outside. Then I killed the brothers and came for the man.

BARB KING: I'm the man in the tower now, and I had nothing to do with the egg.

MIRICAL MAKER: None of us did.

DRAGON: Why are you here?

MAN WHO NEVER MISSES: For you, it seems. To help you get a new egg.

DRAGON lunges, grasps MWNM, kisses him passionately. He struggles at first and then surrenders. She releases him, lifts his palm and licks it.

DRAGON: Salty. You're afraid. *Shoves MWNM away.* I cannot accept a mate who is full of fear.

MAN WHO NEVER MISSES: Fearing a dragon is considered smart in most regions. It's a healthy kind of respect.

DRAGON: Think of the children. A mate who is full of fear will pass his weak seed onto my child. My child will not bear your weak blood. I should snap your head off now to save the world from your progeny, except....

MAN WHO NEVER MISSES: Except?

DRAGON: You smell so strong.

Leans in and sniffs his neck. Grabs necklace.

What's this?

BARB KING: Don't tell me this is part of the ritual?

MYSTERIOUS FIGURE: It's not. She found his musk.

BARB KING: I'm glad someone did.

MAN WHO NEVER MISSES: I freshened up for you. I thought you liked that smell. It's why you came here, right?

DRAGON: Lies! You pretend to be strong.

BARB KING: Mage, that stone spell would be helpful about now.

MIRICAL MAKER: I...

DRAGON: You are weak, fearful, a sheep bleating in the fields.

BARB KING: Anything, mage? Smoke and mirrors?

MIRICAL MAKER: I've forgotten the words.

BARB KING: You what?

MAN WHO NEVER MISSES: Listen, I know you are mad losing your egg and all, but let me help you. I am stronger than you think. Try me.

MYSTERIOUS FIGURE: No, no, no. Are you stupid? Don't challenge her!

DRAGON: I will more than try you! I will roast you slowly and eat your smoking intestines.

MAN WHO NEVER MISSES: Give me a chance. Let me prove to you.

BARB KING: What do you mean you forgot the words?

MIRICAL MAKER: Smoke and mirrors.

BARB KING: When were you going to let me know this? After the dragon ate us?

MIRICAL MAKER: Surprise!

MAN WHO NEVER MISSES: I can be the man of your dreams. I mean, not the kind that steals your egg, because dreams aren't all they're cracked up to be, they are often shattered.

DRAGON: SILENCE! My child has been murdered and you make jokes. Do you take me for a fool to fall for your deceptions?

MYSTERIOUS FIGURE: Don't answer that.

MAN WHO NEVER MISSES: *holds up coin purse.* Look, I have gold. I know you must like gold and, and, *points to the crown*, power. Wealth and power must prove something.

DRAGON: Ha! Such a tiny bag and a tin crown are nothing in comparison to my mound of wealth. I must have someone strong, cunning, viral.

MAN WHO NEVER MISSES: Watch me!

MWNM swings at BK. BK falls over. MWNM looks back at the DRAGON for approval.

DRAGON: Pathetic. You want to impress me.

MAN WHO NEVER MISSES: Trying.

DRAGON: Tear out his heart and eat it.

MF takes out a note pad and scribbles her observations.

MYSTERIOUS FIGURE: Interesting.

BARB KING: Whoa! Whoa! The only woman in this room who can eat my heart is that one. *Points to MF.*

MAN WHO NEVER MISSES: What if I tear out his heart and present it to you? I've ate my quota of hearts. Very filling, though too many and I get heart burn.

DRAGON: Do it.

BARB KING: I don't think so, bitch. You don't come into my castle and order around the hired help.

MAN WHO NEVER MISSES: Hired help? Who are you calling hired help?

BARB KING: I hired you to help kill this bitch, not fuck her. I'm not some exotic creature mating service. Either way, you are failing at both. I begin to question your reputation. They say you never miss, but you've not hit a single mark since you took refuge behind my walls. Here she is. All you do is dance about, avoiding what needs to be done. You can't strike her heart without stringing the bow.

MAN WHO NEVER MISSES: Well I don't see you doing much about it, either? Didn't you want a queen. Well, you have two women here and not a single one is interested in you.

MYSTERIOUS FIGURE: *To MM.* Is that why you are here? It does have a bit of a romantic tone to it.

MIRICAL MAKER: I failed, again. I failed Prince Silverson and now I failed the Tin-crown King. Might as well serve me up for the dragon.

BARB KING: I don't see you sparking any flames with miss eat-your-heart-out. She practically threw herself on you and you shrieked like a little girl. 'I'm not ready. It's all so sudden. Can I have a glass of wine and a moon-light walk.' She's right, you're pathetic. I wouldn't want a weak child, might be the reason your wife died while giving birth.

MAN WHO NEVER MISSES: What the fuck did you say?

BARB KING: She died with your child so she didn't have to bear the shame.

MAN WHO NEVER MISSES: Fuck you. *Throws crown at him.* Fuck you and your tin crown. At least I had a woman's love and didn't have to pay for it. I don't think you are capable of loving anyone but yourself. When you die, no one will mourn you. No one will care. We could walk away and let the dragon eat you and no one would know the difference. Just another pile of bones and ash swept up by the winds of time.

DRAGON: Less talk. More killing.

BARB KING: I mean, she has a point. Since you're not stabbing her one way, stab her another. We outnumber her and could kill her.

MAN WHO NEVER MISSES: A real asshole. I bet if I split you open, there will be saw dust in place of a heart.

BARB KING: More like steel. Cold, hard steel. A pathetic weakling like you wouldn't know a thing about that. I can't believe I hired you. I'll never trust another bard's song again.

MAN WHO NEVER MISSES: The man you hired is in prison, dumb ass. I actually came here to kill you to save him.

DRAGON/MYSTERIOUS FIGURE: Interesting.

BARB KING: You what?

MAN WHO NEVER MISSES: Let me put this in words you understand. Me stabby stabby you. *Draws finger across his throat*. Take head to King Sampson. A real king, not some squatter in a shithole who doesn't know his friends from his enemies.

BARB KING: You want my head? *Draws sword.* Take it if you can.

MAN WHO NEVER MISSES: Let's dance.

Throws coin purse at BK and when he is distracted lunges inside the sword thrust to knock him to the ground. They wrestle, biting, punching etc.

MYSTERIOUS FIGURE: We have to stop this.

MIRICAL MAKER: Why?

DRAGON: Gouge out his eyes, those tasty gooey eyes. I want those first.

MYSTERIOUS FIGURE: If the "King" wins, the Dragon will kill us all.

MIRICAL MAKER: Let's make sure he doesn't.

DRAGON: Don't hit him in the groin! I need that for later.

MYSTERIOUS FIGURE: That would be equally as bad?

MIRICAL MAKER: How so?

DRAGON: You are both pathetic.

Circles around the fight, and easing closer to MM and MF. Sniffs the air.

Something smells, familiar.

MYSTERIOUS FIGURE: Lover Boy kills King Asshole, the dragon gets what she wants, a strong mate to fertilize her egg. See how she's eyeing us. Like cattle in line to be hammered. Once the copulation ends, she will replenish her spent energy by eating us.

MIRICAL MAKER: What do we do?

MYSTERIOUS FIGURE: Do you know any invisibility spells?

MIRICAL MAKER: I do…. but the words are gone, trapped behind the walls of my thick skull.

DRAGON: You! You were in my dreams!

MYSTERIOUS FIGURE: You have to know something.

MIRICAL MAKER: Won't do us any good.

DRAGON: *To MF* You stole my egg!

Dragon begins to arch back and heave forward, transforming into her beast form.

MYSTERIOUS FIGURE: Look, she is transforming back to her original form. If she becomes the dragon, we are all as good as dead.

MIRICAL MAKER: I killed them all. I can't....

MYSTERIOUS FIGURE: *pleading gestures.*

MIRICAL MAKER: Intentions. All about intentions. Prohibere Tempus! *Nothing happens.* See, I told you.

MYSTERIOUS FIGURE: Try again. Please.

BARB KING sits on top of MAN WHO NEVER MISSES, choking him out. DRAGON lets out a loud roar, stopping BK from killing MWNM.

MIRICAL MAKER: Dragon shit. Here goes nothing. Rigescunt Indutae!

Everyone freezes, except MM.

It worked? It worked. The Mirical is back. Hey, oh! *Checks on MF.* Oh no. Oh, dragon shit. Come on. You can't be frozen again. *Tries to move her.* No good. I'll never get her out of here. This is all your fault. *Walks over and kicks BK, injuring foot.* Ouch, owie. *Sits on BK's back and rubs his foot.* I could leave them here. You hear that? *Knocks on BK's head.* I could leave you as statues. Walk away and not a soul would know differently. Some stranger will find the ruins years later and wonder at the life-like stone carvings. I could take a ship to the furthest shores and begin again. Create a new life... the most powerful Mage in another kingdom. Where my failures won't haunt me.

To MWNM. Without you returning with his head, I'm sure your cousin will die in prison. I'm truly sorry for that.

To BK: You won't ever get a queen or build a kingdom, not that you deserve one.

To DRAGON: All this is because someone murdered your egg. I understand your fury, but killing us won't bring you back your progeny. I will try to find the one who did this to you and bring him back for justice.

To MF: You... I think leaving you would be my second greatest failure. I can run away from these three, but... *stands next to her and touches her with his staff.* Molliant Cutis. *Nothing happens.* Molliant Cutis. *Again, nothing.* Don't give up on me now. I guess, there's the way it worked last time. All about the intentions.

Kisses MF. Steps back and waits.

MYSTERIOUS FIGURE: What? You... you did it! You saved us!

MF kisses MM.

MIRICAL MAKER: We can leave now.

71

MYSTERIOUS FIGURE: *gestures to the DRAGON*
What about her?

MIRICAL MAKER: You want to kiss her? I don't feel like having my face torn off.

MYSTERIOUS FIGURE: It's really not fair to leave her. All she wanted was her baby.

MIRICAL MAKER: She needs to move on, realize what is gone is gone and won't be coming back. No use getting all fired up about it.

MYSTERIOUS FIGURE: Like your magic?

MIRICAL MAKER: The magic is still in here. *Touches his head.* Not in here. *Touches his heart.*

MYSTERIOUS FIGURE: What's left in there? *Touches his chest.*

MIRICAL MAKER: Fear.

MYSTERIOUS FIGURE: Is that all?

MIRICAL MAKER: Yes.

MYSTERIOUS FIGURE: Magic is all about intentions, right? There must be something left. Otherwise, I'd still be hard as stone.

MIRICAL MAKER: When I kissed you, I think that was a different kind of magic.

MYSTERIOUS FIGURE: What kind?

MIRICAL MAKER: What do you want to do about the
dragon?

MYSTERIOUS FIGURE: Will the same kind of magic
work on her that you used on me?

MIRICAL MAKER: Way different intentions.

MYSTERIOUS FIGURE: Is there nothing you can do
for her?

MIRICAL MAKER: Nothing *I* can do. Why do you care
so much? She's just a dragon. I'd think you would
want the tin KING, because he can offer you
power, though it may be small and you would
have to live here.

MYSTERIOUS FIGURE: I don't want that ass. He can
stay frozen in time for all I care. It's just that....

MIRICAL MAKER: That what?

MYSTERIOUS FIGURE: You are going to hate me.

MIRICAL MAKER: Are you in love with the dragon?
She does have a dangerous kind of beauty. I don't
think you are the type she needs to fertilize her
egg.

MYSTERIOUS FIGURE: No, I'm the type to break her egg.

MIRICAL MAKER: So, it's true! She was coming to get you. This explains why she didn't kill us right away and why you wanted one of us to woo her for you. Why did you say it was the necromancer?

MYSTERIOUS FIGURE: Much easier to blame a man when he's not here to defend himself.

MIRICAL MAKER: The dragon said a shadow entered her dreams. How could you, unless you...

MF pulls out a wand from her robe.

You're the man in the cloak who sold the tin KING the tower. *Turns back:* You're the necro—! Where did you get that?

MYSTERIOUS FIGURE: I always keep a wand stashed up a sleeve. A girl never knows when she'll need it to protect herself. Yes, I was the man in the cloak, or should I say the woman. After I sold the tower, I was about to leave when I spilled rigor mortis juice on myself.

MIRICAL MAKER: You are very clumsy, aren't you?

MYSTERIOUS FIGURE: Not as much as a man who fumbles his words.

MIRICAL MAKER: You have what you want, why don't you just leave?

MYSTERIOUS FIGURE: Because I don't want to be like you. *Tosses wand onto the ground.* Running away from my problems won't solve anything. It creates more. Free her. Then she can do what she wants with me and leave you all alone. She'll have her vengeance.

MIRICAL MAKER: I won't let you sacrifice yourself. My magic has killed enough people. I won't have another soul on my butcher's bill.

MYSTERIOUS FIGURE: It's my soul and I get to choose what I want to do with it.

MIRICAL MAKER: Then free her yourself.

MYSTERIOUS FIGURE: I don't know how. I only know how to bring back dead things. I know nothing about the living.

MIRICAL MAKER: Why did you steal the dragon's egg?

MYSTERIOUS FIGURE: I wanted to study it, to understand how such a powerful creature emerges from such a fragile source.

MIRICAL MAKER: You didn't kill it to bring it back? An undead dragon under your control.

MYSTERIOUS FIGURE: Half-live dragon. When the egg fell and shattered, I did try. I scooped up as much of the yoke and then I... I couldn't put the pieces together. They wouldn't fit. You know what it's like to destroy so many lives. A slip of the tongue, the twitch of a finger, and so many suffer. When I was younger, I tried my best to put a smile on people's faces. That's what they always said they wanted of me. "You will look prettier if you smiled more. No boy wants to kiss a frowny face." When I smiled, they would all smile back, until I got dirt on my hands and smudged my nose or carried around frogs and lizards, then they'd frown and scold me. "That's not very lady-like. Young ladies who want to marry well don't play with slimy creatures." So, I would release them and observe from afar, longing for their cool scales I was told not to touch. Then the same people would again tell me to smile. I did, though, I learned to fake it. To pretend I was happy so everyone else would be happy. Then one day, a young boy died and the entire village was in mourning and no one smiled. I went to the boy's grave and touched the ground, believing with every fiber in my body that if I could somehow bring him back, everyone would be happy again. Well, the dirt shifted beneath my fingers and clawed hands broke through the ground. A pale face emerged. His eyes, once blue turned gray. I jumped up, full of joy as I helped the boy from his grave. His hands were cold and his body stiff and rigid. I took him to his mother's house, expecting this great outpour of love and relief and ecstatic bliss. What I got were screams and people attacking us with whatever tools were at hand. I escaped with my life, but the boy, they caught him and burned his body. From that day forward, I knew I could never bring people happiness. I gave up trying, but I bring misery instead. My brothers followed me and lost their heads. The egg I wanted to study and return, now smashed, along with the mother's hope for her prodigy. She may be after another, but there's no replacing what I took. Everything I touch dies and no amount of half-life will bring back any joy.

I deserve to die.

MIRICAL MAKER: If we were all to die for our blunders, we'd have to live a million more lifetimes. You're right. We shouldn't run. I have run the world over and look at where I am. The only good I have experienced since that horrific day in the mountains, is meeting you. Call me selfish but I don't want to lose that good, or might as well feed me to the dragon, too.

MYSTERIOUS FIGURE: What do we do?

MIRICAL MAKER: We stay and figure out how to resolve this mess, together.

MYSTERIOUS FIGURE: How?

MIRICAL MAKER: Magic.... Like magic, it is all about intentions.

MYSTERIOUS FIGURE: They all seem intent on killing each other, or all of us.

MIRICAL MAKER: What if we bring them back one by one and convince them otherwise.

MYSTERIOUS FIGURE: I suggest we don't start with her.

MIRICAL MAKER: I was thinking someone less dangerous. This one *points to MWNM,* because he doesn't take risks, unless it is to save someone most dear to him.

MYSTERIOUS FIGURE: Are you going to kiss him, because I won't.

MIRICAL MAKER: No need. *Touches MWNM*. Caro Mitescere.

MAN WHO NEVER MISSES: Huh? What? Who? Where?

MYSTERIOUS FIGURE: You could have done that the entire time. Why did you kiss me?

MIRICAL MAKER: It's all about intentions.

MAN WHO NEVER MISSES: You found your words? Marvelous. I guess we can leave this place. Maybe put up a sign and sell tickets to the show of the millennium. Although, the actors seem a bit stiff and rather boring in those poses. Is there any way we can mold them into something more.... Provocative? Or perhaps leave them as they are and walk away with our skins intact. No, huh? I can tell by the fact that you two are still here that you have thought of that plan. I should be grateful, but in truth, I need his head, and I'm not so sure your good graces will not extend to letting me take his.

MIRICAL MAKER: We need him.

MYSTERIOUS FIGURE: That is to say, she needs him.

MAN WHO NEVER MISSES: You know he threw your brothers' heads in moot.

MYSTERIOUS FIGURE: That asshole!

MIRICAL MAKER: Not helping. We could leave him as a statue and plant flowers around, if you resume your failed courtship with the dragon.

MAN WHO NEVER MISSES: I was never good with the aggressive kind. I have a fear of teeth, claws, and being disemboweled.

MIRICAL MAKER: Then it is agreed. We need your help in persuading the King of the tower that he has met his match.

MYSTERIOUS FIGURE: Ewww, not me.

MAN WHO NEVER MISSES: I guess these two would make a great two backed beast. You owe me, mage. I will need your wit and prestidigitation to rescue my cousin.

MIRICAL MAKER: We live through this and I will walk in and save your cousin myself. Prepare yourselves. I'm going to release him. Caro Mitescere.

BARB KING: Bloody hell! What in the nine wonders have you done, mage? I was all stiff, but now I feel so flaccid. Is this what magic does to a man I'll have none of the—whaaaaa! You did it! You fucking did it, you marvelous man! You got rid of my dragon problem, and look, you even have released my queen to be.

MYSTERIOUS FIGURE: Uh, no.

MAN WHO NEVER MISSES: Oh for two. Try again?

BARB KING: What's this traitor still doing in my home?

MIRICAL MAKER: Listen, King of the tower. The job is not yet finished and quit honestly, only you can finish it.

BARB KING: What do you mean?

MAN WHO NEVER MISSES: You are missing the dragon in the room. Are you blind as well as stupid?

MYSTERIOUS FIGURE: Not helping.

MIRICAL MAKER: You brought us here to help you—

BARB KING: A colossal mistake that I'll never make in the future.

MIRICAL MAKER: And I have found a solution for most of your problems.

BARB KING: Most, huh?

MYSTERIOUS FIGURE: Count me out of any of your plans.

BARB KING: I see. Continue, mage.

MIRICAL MAKER: I present to you, your new queen.

BARB KING: I don't know. Do you think she would accept me?

MYSTERIOUS FIGURE: You are just her type. Strong, virial, fearless, and a king!

MAN WHO NEVER MISSES: What more could a woman, or even a dragon want?

MIRICAL MAKER: This is your one true shot of being rid of the two issues, plus us three. Then you can live here in your tower happily ever after.

MAN WHO NEVER MISSES: What man could boast he has a dragon for a wife and not be forced to sleep on a cot for the rest of his days?

BARB KING: What do I have to do?

MIRICAL MAKER: What you do best. Kiss her with every intention of freeing her. Kiss her like you want her to melt at your touch. Kiss her like there's nothing more important in your life.

BARB KING: I got this. I am an expert at soften woman to the fire of my kisses.

MYSTERIOUS FIGURE: I've had better.

BARB KING: Whelp, here goes everything.

BK kisses DRAGON

MAN WHO NEVER MISSES: Think she'll fall for him?

MYSTERIOUS FIGURE: If she doesn't, we are back in the same position we were to start. I just hope she can forgive me.

MAN WHO NEVER MISSES: For what?

MIRICAL MAKER: Story is too long for a recap.

Mysterious FIGURE: I dropped the egg.

MAN WHO NEVER MISSES: Oh, that's not so good, er I mean, how long can a dragon hold a grudge?

MYSTERIOUS FIGURE: My guys is a few millennia, or until my bones are digested.

DRAGON: Such virality, such strength, such power.

MIRICAL MAKER: So far so good.

DRAGON: What is she still doing here? She stalked me in my slumber, stolen my egg and murdered my child! She must die!

MYSTERIOUS FIGURE: All you accuse me of I am guilty. My intentions were never to harm your egg. I wanted to study it, to better understand your kind so I can convince people to leave you all in peace, since there are so few of you left. I committed a grievous error and I—

BARB KING: —have found you a stronger mate. A simple drop and the egg broke. Must mean the dragon inside would break easy as well. I promise you, iron runs through my blood and I will provide you a dragon child that is no match for any that has ever lived. The blood of a king will course through its veins.

DRAGON: I see, but she should be punished.

BARB KING: Oh, I agree. I have the perfect punishment. You see, this lovely tower used to be her home. So I say to you, vile creature, you are banished, never to set one foot on this stone else you will be burnt to ash and that ash swept away into the latrine where it shall be forever shat upon!

DRAGON: I like that.

MYSTERIOUS FIGURE: I accept this decry, though it tears my heart to leave my lovely home.

BARB KING: So, will you be my dragon queen forever more?

DRAGON: I accept you as a suitable mate, unlike that limp fish.

MAN WHO NEVER MISSES: I've been called worse.

BARB KING: Then I declare you Queen of my region, and my heart.

MAN WHO NEVER MISSES: Since you got what want. Will you still honor your pledge?

BARB KING: Yes, of course. I'd be a bad king to start off everything with lies.

MWNM steps up to BK, like an embrace, but draws BK's sword.

MAN WHO NEVER MISSES: Sorry. I'm going to need this head to save my cousin's. I mean, it's the only way. King Sampson made it clear that if I played any other tricks, my kin was as good as worm's meat.

BARB KING: I need my head and you can't have it.

MAN WHO NEVER MISSES: So, you are going back on your word. What head will I take back?

BARB KING: I'm sure any head will do.

MYSTERIOUS FIGURE: I got it!

MF exits.

DRAGON: You can have his after I have his.

BARB KING: I thought you were on my side.

DRAGON: I was going to eat you the moments after you fertilized my egg.

BARB KING: Oh, I guess we can work that detail out after I wed and bed you. Then I will be the one eating—

MF enters, carrying a bag with a head in it.

MYSTERIOUS FIGURE: Here, take this bag—

MAN WHO NEVER MISSES: I'm sure the head in here is much prettier than the one Sampson expects.

MYSTERIOUS FIGURE: The hot sun has shriveled it up. May it be more useful to you dead than he was to me alive.

MIRICAL MAKER: You are the first necromancer in history to resurrect a life before it was dead.

MYSTERIOUS FIGURE: I might be of the mind for a career change, if the right teacher comes along.

MIRICAL MAKER: I believe I can take an apprentice, if I remember all the right words.

MYSTERIOUS FIGURE: So far you have.

MIRICAL MAKER: I guess miracles really do happen.

MAN WHO NEVER MISSES: If you two are done making googly-eyes at one another, I am also calling in your debt, mage. I helped you.

MIRICAL MAKER: No more than a hole in a bucket helps hold water.

MAN WHO NEVER MISSES: At least I didn't interfere, but I require your services in case this trick fails, I may need you to make another king disappear and free my cousin.

MYSTERIOUS FIGURE: If all else fails, I can always bring him back to half-life.

MAN WHO NEVER MISSES: How reassuring.

DRAGON: What are you still doing here? Get out. Out of my tower!

MAN WHO NEVER MISSES: The lady of the house has spoken!

Exit MF, MM, and MWNM

BARB KING: Where were we, my love?

DRAGON: Deciding on who gets eaten first.

Blackout

End of Play

Made in the USA
Monee, IL
28 April 2022